For Martha, a kindred spirit and a great friend — M.F.

Text © 2015 Maureen Fergus
Illustrations © 2015 Qin Leng

Owlkids Books acknowledges the financial support of the Canada Council for the Arts, the Ontario Arts Council, the Government of Canada through the Canada Book Fund (CBF) and the Government of Ontario through the Ontario Media Development Corporation's Book Initiative for our publishing activities.

Published in Canada by
Owlkids Books Inc.
10 Lower Spadina Avenue
Toronto, ON M5V 2Z2

Published in the United States by
Owlkids Books Inc.
1700 Fourth Street
Berkeley, CA 94710

Library and Archives Canada Cataloguing in Publication

Fergus, Maureen, author
    And what if I won't? / written by Maureen Fergus ; illustrated by Qin Leng.

ISBN 978-1-77147-065-0 (bound)

    I. Leng, Qin, illustrator II. Title.

PS8611.E735A64 2015   jC813'.6   C2014-904544-1

Library of Congress Control Number: 2014945831

Edited by: Jessica Burgess
Designed by: Alisa Baldwin

Manufactured in Shenzhen, Guangdong, China, in October 2014, by WKT Co. Ltd.
Job #14B1014

A   B   C   D   E   F

Publisher of Chirp, chickaDEE and OWL
www.owlkidsbooks.com

MAUREEN FERGUS

QIN LENG

And What If I Won't ?

Owlkids Books

"Benny, please put your plate in the sink."

"What would you do if I said no?" asked Benny.

"I'd tell you that just saying no is rude," replied his mom. "Then I'd explain why it's important to help out around the house."

"Well," said Benny, "what would you do if I said that I liked being rude, that I didn't care about helping out around the house, and then I chucked my plate across the room?"

"I guess I'd try to catch the plate before it hit the wall," said his mom.

"But what would you do if you couldn't catch it?" asked Benny.

"And it smashed into the wall, you mean?" said his mom.

"Exactly!" said Benny.

"I'd make you clean up the mess, of course."

"But what would you do if I refused to clean up the mess?" asked Benny. "What would you do if I made an even BIGGER mess—so big that I practically destroyed the kitchen?"

"If you destroyed the kitchen, Benny, I'm afraid I'd have to give you a time-out," said his mom regretfully.

"What would you do if instead of staying in time-out, I ran around the house drawing on the walls with permanent marker?" asked Benny.

"What would you do if I put on my muddy rain boots and jumped on the couch?"

"What would you do if I purposely tore pages out of library books?"

"If you did that," gasped his mom,
"I'd give you to the zoo!"

"But what would you do if the zookeeper said she didn't want me anymore because I bit her when she tried to feed me and I made horrible faces at people when they tried to take pictures of me and I roared at the baby penguins whenever they splashed at me?"

"The poor penguins!" cried his mom. "Oh, Benny, how could you be so cruel?"

Instead of answering, Benny laughed like an evil genius. Then he stopped laughing and said, "Well? What would you do?"

"If the zookeeper didn't want you, I suppose I'd have no choice but to sell you to the circus," sighed his mom.

"Really?" said Benny. "But what would you do if I put sand in the cotton-candy machine and tied the lions' tails together and pulled down the clowns' pants so that everybody could see their polka-dotted underwear?"

"What would you do if the ringmaster showed up at the front door
and said he'd had enough of me?"

"I'd do the only thing a loving mother can do when her son is being so monstrously naughty that even a circus won't keep him," said Benny's mom sadly. "I'd send you to the moon."

Even though Benny kind of liked the idea of being sent to the moon, he didn't stop there. "But what would you do if instead of flying to the moon like I was supposed to, I shouted bad words at the people in Mission Control, zoomed across the galaxy, and crash-landed on a planet filled with aliens?"

"I'd weep bitterly at the news that you'd
shouted bad words, laugh joyfully at the
news that you'd landed safely, and then—"

"Hire a space taxi to come and get me?"
suggested Benny.

"No," said his mom. "Then I'd
tell the aliens to keep you."

Benny laughed again. Then he climbed up onto his mom's lap and whispered, "Mom, what would you do if I was SOOOO naughty that the aliens didn't want to keep me? What would you do if they used a giant alien slingshot to hurl me back to earth, and I landed right smack in the middle of our very own front yard?"

"I'd give you a big hug," replied his mom. "I'd tell you how much I'd missed you and how much I love you…"

"…and then I'd ask you to please put your plate in the sink."